POTATO CHIP BO

SO GOOD YOU CAN'T STOP READING THEM!

Time to Get Up!

Written by
Marilyn Pitt & Jane Hileman
Illustrated by John Bianchi

You have to get up now.

I don't want to get up.

Where are you?
Are you up?

ZZZ
7:50

Come down and eat. Are you up?

ZZZ

Where is he?
Go get him, dog.

No. Get
down, dog.

Not now.
Get down.

Where are they?

Z Z Z